A DROP OF HONEY

To my darling little granddaughter, Emma
D.B.

To the memory of Zabel
and the children lost in the earthquake of 1988
A.K.

SIMON AND SCHUSTER BOOKS FOR YOUNG READERS
Simon & Schuster Building, Rockefeller Center
1230 Avenue of the Americas, New York, New York 10020

10 9 8 7 6 5 4 3 2 1
Library of Congress Cataloging-in-Publication Data
Bider, Djemma. A drop of honey. Summary: After being bad-tempered with her brothers, Anayida falls asleep and
dreams of the terrible things that can happen because of the spilling of a single drop honey.   [1. Folkore—Armenia]
I. Kojoyian, Armen, ill. II. Title.   PZ8.1.B527Dr   1988   398.2'08991992 [E]   87-32323
ISBN 0-671-66265-1

A DROP OF HONEY

◆◆◆

AN ARMENIAN TALE

by Djemma Bider
illustrated by Armen Kojoyian

Simon and Schuster Books for Young Readers
Published by Simon & Schuster Inc., New York

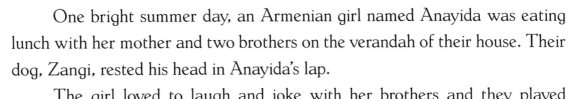

One bright summer day, an Armenian girl named Anayida was eating lunch with her mother and two brothers on the verandah of their house. Their dog, Zangi, rested his head in Anayida's lap.

The girl loved to laugh and joke with her brothers and they played together all day during the summer. But today, for no special reason, Anayida's big, black eyes were sad. She was feeling cross and she ate very slowly. Her brothers ate their lunch in one quick gulp and began to pester her.

"Anayida, won't you hurry a little? We want to go swimming. We can't wait all day for you."

Now, on any other day, Anayida would have hurried along to please her impatient brothers, but this day she said sourly, "You can just wait until I am ready. The river won't run away."

"What do you think you are, a princess?" said one of her brothers. "Girls are so much trouble. So will you hurry up?"

"No" said Anayida.

As soon as her brothers heard this, they ran off without her, shoving each other as they hurried down the path to the river. Zangi, yelping with excitement, bounded along after them.

Anayida called after her brothers, "Rouben, Gegan, wait for me. Bad boys! Come back at once!" But they did not look back at Anayida, and she was left behind.

Stroking her daughter's glossy black hair, Anayida's mother said gently, "Why don't you run after your brothers? They want you to go to the river, too. They were just too excited to wait any longer."

"Oh no! I won't go at all. They'll be sorry. They won't have any fun unless I'm there!" And with big tears in her eyes, Anayida scolded on and on.

"Don't let trifles spoil your day, my child," said Anayida's mother, putting her arm around her. "Remember, a small quarrel may lead to big trouble. Now, I must leave for the vineyard." She took her wicker basket and with a parting kiss, walked off toward the long rows of vines growing on the hillside.

Anayida finished eating at last. She sat quietly, staring into the distance. Down the hill, the river showed blue through the trees. Far beyond the river she could see the mountains. The day was very, very hot. Anayida felt drowsy.

A yellow spot on the wooden table caught her eye. It was a drop of honey. She knew she should wash it away, because it would soon attract bees. But it was such a hot day that she didn't want to move. She put her hands on the table and rested her head on them. Her long braids fell down around her face. She looked at the yellow spot. As she watched, it seemed to grow larger and larger.

Anayida dreamed she had a basket over her arm and she was going to the market in the nearby village. Zangi, with his long tongue hanging out, was running happily after her. Anayida had decided to buy the ingredients needed for baklava—a wonderful baked dessert made from layers of light, crisp pastry and filled with delicious nuts and spices.

"I am going to help my mother bake baklava," she said to the smiling merchant, a tall man who sold nuts from a cart under a canopy. The nut seller helped Anayida select some fine almonds, walnuts, and pistachios. He patted Zangi and scratched the dog behind his ears.

The dairy lady sold Anayida a blue-and-white crock of sweet, yellow butter. The shelves and counters of her stand were piled with yellow and white cheeses, some round, some square, some long like sausages. The cheeses smelled very good to Zangi.

Next, Anayida stepped into the tiny shop of the spice merchant to buy cinnamon bark and dried lemon peel. This store was her favorite, because it held so many good smells. Anayida smelled nutmeg, cloves, and pickling spices. There were different kinds of paprika, and many fascinating scents she could not name. Zangi did not like the smell of spices. He waited outside. Anayida put the cinnamon bark and the lemon peel in her basket and said goodbye to the spice merchant.

"Now then, do I have everything I need?" she asked herself.

Just then she saw a large woman with many gold chains around her neck standing near a small cart. "Best sweet-scented honey! Straight from the honeycomb!" the woman cried. "Hurry, hurry while it lasts!"

"Oh my goodness! The most important thing—honey! I almost forgot to get honey," said Anayida to herself. She walked toward the honey woman, who at this moment was pouring honey from one clay jar to another. Like a golden gem, a thick drop of honey fell from the jar onto a cobblestone.

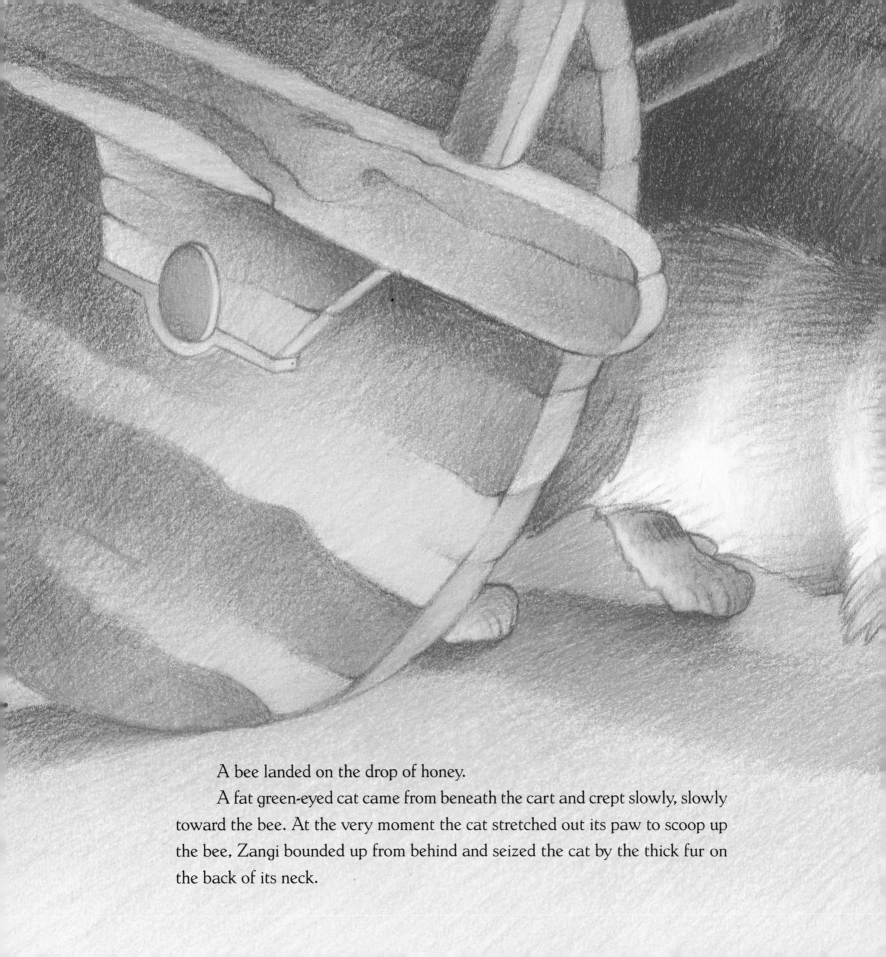

A bee landed on the drop of honey.

A fat green-eyed cat came from beneath the cart and crept slowly, slowly toward the bee. At the very moment the cat stretched out its paw to scoop up the bee, Zangi bounded up from behind and seized the cat by the thick fur on the back of its neck.

Anayida went running to Zangi to free the cat, but just then, the honey woman looked up and saw Zangi struggling with the cat.

"Don't you touch my cat you wicked dog! Help! Help!" she screamed. Her husband, who was an old man with a long beard, came running with a stick.

All the dogs of the marketplace wanted to see what was happening to their good friend Zangi. They jumped and barked and made a terrible racket. People came running and pushing from all directions to see what was the matter. Someone accidently tipped over a pyramid of crockery pots displayed for sale on the cobblestones of the market square. Counters were knocked down. Watermelons, apricots, peaches, and pomegranates were scattered about everywhere. Zangi and his friends forgot about the cat and fought over the spilled sausages. The shouts, screams, and crashing noises grew louder and louder. And more people came to join the fight.

Anayida's basket fell to the ground. Her beautiful, brightly colored dress caught on a hook and was torn. She tried to run away. Market women with wooden ladles in their hands, shopkeepers, farmers, and housewives all began to chase her. Even the old men left their games of checkers to join the chase.

"Mama, mama, help me!" Anayida cried.

"Wake up, my darling, wake up!" And there was Anayida's mother holding her in her arms at the table on the verandah of their own home. Anayida was still saying, "Honey....Zangi....My beautiful dress...." And then, completely awake, she said, "Oh, mama, thank goodness it was only a dream! Now I can still go swimming with Rouben and Gegan." Anayida threw her arms around her mother and hugged and kissed her.

Her mother smiled. "What has made you change your mind about swimming, Anayida?" she asked.

"I'll tell you all about it later," said Anayida. "If only you knew what terrible things can happen because of just one drop of honey!" And then, thinking for a moment, she said, "You know, mama, you were so right about small quarrels leading to big troubles."

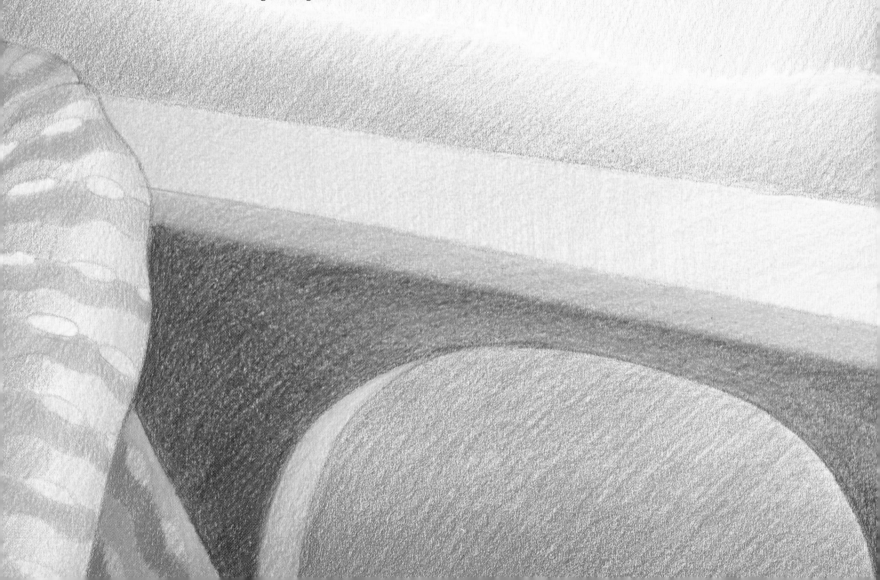

Anayida ran happily to the river.

Anayida's Baklava

Pastry

17 sheets phyllo pastry, each approximately 12 by 12 inches

¹/₂ cup melted sweet butter

Filling

Combine:

1¹/₂ cups pistachios, walnuts, and almonds, finely chopped and mixed

2 slices dried pineapple sliced into small pieces (if desired)

¹/₄ cup raisins (if desired)

2 tablespoons sugar

¹/₂ teaspoon ground cinnamon

Syrup

¹/₂ cup honey

¹/₂ cup sugar

¹/₂ cup water

1 cinnamon stick

1 teaspoon freshly squeezed lemon juice

Preheat oven to 350°.

Allow pastry leaves to warm to room temperature. Brush a 12-inch baking pan with some of the melted butter. Place 2 sheets of the phyllo into the pan, brushing each with melted butter. Repeat for the next 12 sheets, brushing some with the butter, and spreading others evenly with filling. Brush the last 3 sheets of phyllo with butter only. Bake for 30 minutes at 350°, then increase temperature to 450° and bake for a further 5 minutes, or until golden.

Meanwhile, prepare the syrup. In a small saucepan, combine the syrup ingredients and bring to a boil, stirring constantly. Reduce the heat and simmer uncovered for about 30 minutes. Remove from the heat and keep warm.

When done, remove the baklava from the oven and cut it into diamond-shaped pieces with a sharp knife. Spoon the syrup evenly over the baklava. Serve at room temperature.

Makes 10 servings.